Dick King-Smith

Under the Mishmash Trees

Illustrated by Seb Burnett

PUFFIN

PUFFIN BOOKS

Published by the Penguin Group
Penguin Books Ltd, 80 Strand, London WC2R 0RL, England
Penguin Group (USA) Inc., 375 Hudson Street, New York, New York 10014, USA
Penguin Books Australia Ltd, 250 Camberwell Road, Camberwell, Victoria 3124, Australia
Penguin Books Canada Ltd, 10 Alcorn Avenue, Toronto, Ontario, Canada M4V 3B2
Penguin Books India (P) Ltd, 11 Community Centre, Panchsheel Park, New Delhi – 110 017, India
Penguin Books (NZ) Ltd, Cnr Rosedale and Airborne Roads, Albany, Auckland, New Zealand
Penguin Books (South Africa) (Pty) Ltd, 24 Sturdee Avenue, Rosebank 2196, South Africa

Penguin Books Ltd, Registered Offices: 80 Strand, London WC2R 0RL, England

www.penguin.com

First published 2005
1

Text copyright © Fox Busters Ltd, 2005
Illustrations copyright © Seb Burnett, 2005
All rights reserved

The moral right of the author and illustrator has been asserted

Set in 17/22.25pt Perpetua
Made and printed in England by Clays Ltd, St Ives plc

British Library Cataloguing in Publication Data
A CIP catalogue record for this book is available from the British Library
ISBN 0-141-31768-X

Chapter One

'If there's one creature I can't stand,'
said Og, 'it's a slobbadunk.'

Og was a gombrizil. All gombrizils
have very short names and very long
legs. Slobbadunks, on the other hand,
have very long names and no legs at all.

Generally speaking, gombrizils get
along quite well with slobbadunks, but

Og was the exception.

'I can't stick 'em,' he said to Ut, his wife, as they stood side by side under the mishmash trees. 'They make me feel physically sick.'

'I know, dear,' said Ut. 'Perhaps you were frightened by one when you were very small. None of the rest of us mind them; they're harmless. Look, here's one coming along now, it won't hurt you.'

'Ugh!' cried Og. 'Horrible thing! Hold my leg, Ut, I'm scared!'

Ut wrapped two of her seven long legs round one of Og's as the slobbadunk approached very slowly, sliding along on its huge stomach. It was staring at Og with the one large green eye in the middle of its forehead. It opened its

round rubbery mouth and burped. Og
began to cry.

'Go away!' shouted Ut to the
slobbadunk. 'You are frightening my
husband.'

The slobbadunk slithered to a halt.

'Sorry,' it said in a very deep voice. It
burped again. 'Must be something I ate,'

it said. 'I'm a martyr to indigestion. It runs in the family: we all suffer from wind, all us Wollycobbles. By the way, allow me to introduce myself. My name is Tumblerum Wollycobble.'

'Are you a boy or a girl?' asked Ut.

'Both, madam,' said the slobbadunk.

'Most of us are.'

It spoke so politely to the two
gombrizils that Ut felt she should tell
it her name in return; so she did.

'Ut what?' asked Tumblerum
Wollycobble.

'Just Ut.'

'Oh. And your husband's name?'

'Og.'

'Og what?'

'Just Og.'

'Why is he crying, madam?' asked the slobbadunk.

'He's scared of you,' said Ut.

'But we're quite harmless.'

'Yes, I know,' said Ut, 'but the fact remains that Og can't stand slobbadunks.'

'Oh,' said Tumblerum Wollycobble.

There was a hurt look in its green eye, Ut could see, and once again it opened its round rubbery mouth as if to say something more, but all that came out was another belch. Then it slithered away – rather sadly, Ut thought.

But Og, seeing it depart, became brave and started shouting rude things after it, like 'Windbag!' and 'Smellybreath!'

Ut unwrapped the two legs with which she had been holding her husband.

'I'll tell you something, Og,' she said. 'You are not a very nice gombrizil. I've a good mind to divorce you.'

'Feel free,' said Og. 'I can soon find another wife.'

Ut stood up very tall on her seven long legs, staring angrily at Og out of her

three stalky eyes. Female gombrizils are quite a bit bigger than the males, and for a moment it looked as though Og might live to regret his words. But just then a noisy flock of strollops flew into the nearby mishmash trees.

Strollops are great carriers of news, especially bad news. Looking down in flight, they see everything that is going on below, and they tell the world about it in their shrill voices. Seldom can any creature do anything without the strollops knowing, and even a minor accident is loudly reported.

Now they perched in the tops of the mishmash trees, screeching loudly, but Ut and Og were too angry with one another to listen to their message.

'Trouble!' squawked the strollops. 'The slobbadunk's in trouble!'

Chapter Two

Ut turned away and flounced off in the direction that Tumblerum Wollycobble had taken, and Og went off the opposite way, sulkily.

Ut made her way through the trees, moving jerkily as all gombrizils do. Six of their seven legs stick out, three a side, rather like the oars of a rowing boat. The seventh, which is much the largest, grows beneath their chins.

With this seventh leg Ut reached out, planting the claw on its end firmly into the ground ahead, to pull herself forward. At the same time she sculled with all the other six legs together, which resulted in a kind of huge hop.

No one can say that gombrizils are graceful, but they can move remarkably

quickly if necessary, as when pursuing various small creatures on which they feed, such as spuddicks, swoots or filigogs.

Ut was in fact not hungry at this moment, but angry – with herself. *Silly me*, she thought as she hopped along, *talking about divorce like that; the last thing I want really. I don't want to lose Og, he's so handsome. I just wish he wasn't so beastly to slobbadunks. Not only is he nasty to them, he's frightened of them too, silly boy.*

Just then Ut heard, not far ahead, a sudden loud deep voice.

'Help!' it called. 'Help me, please, someone!'

That's Tumblerum Wollycobble, she thought, and she hopped her fastest until

she came to a meadow of slippysloppy
grass, in the middle of which lay the fat
figure of the slobbadunk. As it heard Ut
approaching, its round rubbery mouth
opened.

'I don't know who you are,' it said,
'but could you help me?'

'I'm Ut,' said Ut, 'the gombrizil. Don't
you remember me?'

'Oh, madam!' cried the slobbadunk. 'Of course I remember you. How could I ever forget you? But I shall never again see your kind face.'

'Why not?' asked Ut.

'Because, madam,' said Tumblerum Wollycobble, 'I have been struck blind! It happened so suddenly. One minute I could see as clearly as usual, the next I could see nothing! Alas, I have lost the use of my eye, my only eye.'

Ut drew closer and looked carefully at the middle of the slobbadunk's forehead. There was indeed no sign of that one green eye, and Ut could now see why. The meadow of slippysloppy grass was a very wet one and, somehow, a lump of mud, thrown up perhaps by an extra large belch as the slobbadunk grazed, had landed on its eye and blanked out its sight.

But before Ut could say anything, a torrent of words burst from Tumblerum Wollycobble's round rubbery mouth.

'Oh, madam!' it cried. 'What a sorry slobbadunk am I! Never again shall I see your kindly face or that of your noble husband. Never again shall I see the happy hopping of the bushy-tailed filigogs, nor the long ears of the spuddicks, nor the soft shells of the hagafists. Never again shall I see the strollops flying up to perch and preen and pick the freeble fruits from the mishmash trees.'

'Rubbish!' laughed Ut. 'You will see all those things.'

'But, madam,' said the slobbadunk, 'I
have lost the sight of my eye!'

'No you haven't,' said Ut, 'you've just
got mud in it. Keep still now and I'll get
it out for you,' and with her big seventh
leg she began, very carefully, to wipe
away the mud on the middle of the
slobbadunk's forehead. Soon she saw a

glint of colour, and before long, the one large green eye was clean and clear again.

Tumblerum Wollycobble opened its round rubbery mouth.

'I can see again!' it cried. 'I can see you, but how can I ever thank you enough? If ever I can do you a favour, please call upon me, madam.'

'Oh, do call me Ut.'

'I hardly think I can, madam. You are, after all, a gombrizil, and gombrizils are septipedal.'

'What's that mean?' asked Ut.

'Having seven legs,' said the slobbadunk. 'While I, like all my kind, am an apode.'

'What's that mean?'

'No legs. Therefore vastly inferior to an animal such as yourself, madam.'

'Oh, but that's nonsense,' said Ut. 'Legs don't matter, it's brains that count, and you've obviously got lots, knowing such difficult words as those.'

The slobbadunk's answer to this was a loud belch.

'I beg your pardon, madam,' it said. 'I would willingly exchange what brains I have for a decent digestion. When your husband called me "Windbag" and "Smellybreath", I fear that he was speaking the truth.'

'It was very rude of him,' said Ut, 'and I told him so.'

'Think nothing of it,' said Tumblerum. 'As I told you, we Wollycobbles all suffer in the same way, and I myself suffer worst of all.' And as if to prove it, it let off a long string of burps.

This noise disturbed a family of filigogs that had been hiding among the slippysloppy grass, and they hopped hastily away, their bushy tails curled over their hairy backs.

Gombrizils are very partial to filigogs, especially tender hairless little ones, and with her sharp-taloned seventh leg Ut quickly speared three and popped them into her mouth.

'Sorry,' she said to the slobbadunk when she had swallowed them, 'I should have offered you one.'

'No use to me, madam,' said Tumblerum. 'All slobbadunks are herbivores.'

'What's that mean?' asked Ut.

'Vegetarians. We do not eat meat.'

'Oh, poor you!' said Ut. 'What do you eat then?'

'Slippysloppy grass,' said the slobbadunk, and it opened its round rubbery mouth and sucked in a great deal of the stuff.

'No wonder it gets indigestion,' said Ut to herself, 'shovelling down all that slimy muck. Herbivore indeed! What it

needs is something solid, like one of
those filigogs. Or better still, a couple
of nice fat swoots.' And being of a
soft-hearted nature, she set off to see
if she could find some.

Swoots as a rule live under large flat
stones, and Ut, using one or other of her
seven legs, turned over a number until
she found a colony of swoots: shiny pink,
sausage-shaped creatures that wriggled

 and wiggled in alarm at being suddenly exposed to the light.

Quickly Ut speared and ate all but the two biggest swoots. These she carefully stowed in the useful little pouch that all gombrizils have upon their chests. Then she made her way  back to the slobbadunk, guided, of course, by the sound of its ceaseless burping.

'Tumblerum,' she said.

'Yes, madam?'

'I can call you Tumblerum, can I?'

'Of course.'

'It's rather a long name. We gombrizils

are used to short ones. Could I perhaps call you Tum?'

'Certainly.'

'Right,' said Ut. 'Now listen, Tum. Open your mouth and shut your eye, and I'll give you something as nice as pie.'

Obediently, Tumblerum Wollycobble closed its one green eye and opened its round rubbery mouth.

Quick as a flash, Ut reached into her pouch with her seventh leg, speared one of the swoots, popped it between the slobbadunk's rubbery lips, and tickled it under its chin (or where its chin would have been if it had had one) to make it swallow.

Which it did.

Alarmed and horrified at the feeling of the soft slimy swoot slipping down its throat, the slobbadunk opened its mouth again to protest, whereupon Ut popped in the second swoot.

'There,' she said. 'Unless I miss my guess, that should do the trick, Tum. No need for you to get the wind up any more.'

Chapter Three

Ut went hopping back to the grove of
mishmash trees, in whose branches the
strollops sat screeching noisily. Beneath
the trees, Ut could see Og still looking
sulky.

'Og, darling,' said Ut quietly, 'I'm
perfectly serious about something. You
are going to come with me and apologize

to that slobbadunk to which you were so rude.'

'Never!' shouted Og.

Ut took one huge hop that landed her beside her smaller husband.

She raised her seventh leg and two others for good measure, in a manner that was distinctly threatening.

'Og,' she said. 'You will do as I say. Or else.'

Og sighed. 'You've got to hand it to the old girl,' he said to himself. 'She's the one with bottle. Scared of nothing, she is.' He sighed again. *Not like me*, he thought. *Frightened of slobbadunks!*

'Come on then,' said Ut.

At that moment they heard a deep voice calling.

'Madam! Madam!' cried the voice, and then they saw, slithering slowly towards them, the sinuous shape of Tumblerum Wollycobble, the slobbadunk.

'Madam!' it cried again.

'Oh, no!' said Og, and he turned, poised for flight, but Ut stuck the claw of her seventh leg in his pouch, making him prisoner.

'Now's your chance,' she said to him,

and to the slobbadunk, 'Come here,
Tum, old boy . . . er, old girl . . . er, old
thing. My husband has something to say
to you.'

'Oh, madam!' said Tumblerum. 'It is I
who have something to say to you!
Thank you, madam, thank you from the
bottom of my heart and the bottom of
my stomach and the bottom of my
bottom! Listen, please.'

They listened for quite a long time,
but no further sound came from the
slobbadunk's round rubbery mouth.

'What do you hear?' it said at last.

'Nothing,' said Ut and Og together.

'Exactly! What would you have expected
to hear?'

'Burps!' cried Ut. 'Oh, you're not

burping any more! Those swoots did the trick!'

'They did,' said Tumblerum. 'Thanks to them, I am a martyr to indigestion no longer.'

'You're a vegetarian no longer either,' said Ut. 'Swoots are good red meat, no doubt of that, so you can't call yourself a herbivore any more.'

'I don't care!' cried Tumblerum Wollycobble. 'Because of you, my troubles are over. I'm the happiest slobbadunk in the world, and you, madam, are the kindest, cleverest gombrizil, and your husband is the most handsome and, no doubt, the bravest. How sorry I am, sir, that you should not care for slobbadunks. Your lady wife said that you are

frightened of us, but that I simply cannot
believe. How could a brave gentleman
like yourself possibly be scared of a
humble creature such as myself?'

Og's three eyes had been out on stalks
anyway at the sight of the slobbadunk,
but now they began to glisten with
pleasure at being called handsome and
brave.

'Scared?' he said. 'Me? Of you? What an idea!'

'Great!' said Ut. 'Well, if you're not scared of my friend Tum, you can stay here with him . . . er, with her . . . er, with it, while I go off and collect a pouchful of swoots. But before I go, let me remind you, Og, that there's one word I haven't yet heard you say to Tum.' And she waved her seventh leg somewhat menacingly at her husband.

'What?' said Og.

'Oh,' he said.

'Oh, yes,' he said, and then, to the

slobbadunk, 'Sorry for calling you names.'

'Think nothing of it, sir,' said Tumblerum Wollycobble as Ut hopped off. 'Sticks and stones may break my bones (or they would if I had any bones), but words will never hurt me. Still, it's most kind of you to apologize.'

A silence fell beneath the mishmash trees, in which the strollops, now full of freeble fruits, slept. A pair of soft-shelled hagafists came out of their burrow and began to graze on the succulent slippysloppy grass.

Tumblerum lay still, waiting for Ut to bring it more swoots.

Og stood stiffly on his seven legs, wondering what to say next to this slobbadunk that, he found, no longer revolted him. 'In fact,' he said to himself, 'now I come to think, it's not such a bad sort of beast.'

At last he said, 'Nice weather for the time of year, eh? Warm. Dry. No wind.'

'No wind!' replied Tumblerum Wollycobble happily. 'How right you are, sir!'

At this moment Ut reappeared, her pouch crammed with wriggling swoots. Quickly she speared one and popped it into the slobbadunk's round rubbery mouth. She felt particularly pleased with life. Her stomach was full, for while swoot-hunting, she had caught and eaten a large long-eared spuddick (one of her favourite meals, they were so juicy), and now here was her husband happily

conversing with her friend Tum. Only
one thing was needed to make things
perfect.

'Og, darling,' she said sweetly. 'Do you
love me?'

Og looked at her. He was pleased with
life too. *How brave I am*, he thought, *I'm
not frightened of slobbadunks any more.*

'Yes, old girl,' he said. 'I suppose I do.'

'And you like Tum and you're going to

be friends with it?'

'Yes, old girl,' said Og. 'I suppose I could.'

'Goody, goody!' cried Ut. 'Here, have a swoot. Tum won't mind, will you, Tum?'

'Oh, no, madam.'

'You'd better have another one yourself.'

'If you please, madam. If sir doesn't object?'

'Of course not, Wollycobble, my friend,' said Og. 'Always remember to do what my wife tells you, and everything will be all right.'

'Yes, sir,' said the Slobbadunk.

It turned its head to face Ut and she saw its one green eye shut in a big wink.

Chapter Four

From then on the life of Og and Ut
under the mishmash trees changed, for
Tumblerum Wollycobble came to live
there too. Ut, after all, had to catch
swoots for it and she didn't want to go
looking all over the place to find it,
especially as it was now burp-free and so
much harder to track down.

Og had made quite a friend of Tum, possibly because he liked being called handsome and brave and being treated in a most respectful way. He was now more kindly disposed to slobbadunks in general and to this one in particular.

Tumblerum was, of course, in seventh heaven at being treated so nicely by these wonderful gombrizils.

'I cannot thank you enough, madam,' it said to Ut, 'for all your trouble in catching swoots for me. I only wish there was some favour I might do for you in return.'

'There may be, one day, Tum,' Ut replied.

In fact, that day was not long in coming.

An interesting fact about gombrizils is

that they cannot have babies when they
are young, but must wait until they are
middle-aged, which Ut now was.

One morning she came back from
swoot-hunting to find Og and Tum side
by side under the mishmash trees. She
emptied her pouch and left them eating
happily.

Then she went off into a quiet corner and began to make a nest of mishmash leaves.

A little later she came back and said to her husband, 'Can you spare a minute, Og?'

'Of course,' he replied. 'What is it?'

'This,' said Ut, and she led him to the nest. There in the middle was a large bright-blue egg.

'You are to be a father,' she said.

'Wonderful!' shouted Og, and he scratched her (gently) with his seventh leg.

'Let's tell Tum!' he said.

When Tumblerum heard the glad news, its one green eye glistened with tears of joy. Most slobbadunks cannot

have children, but Tum was so pleased
for its new friends.

'Tum,' said Ut. 'Do you remember
saying you'd like to do me a favour one
day?'

'Indeed I do, madam.'

'Well, you see,' said Ut, 'I'm going to
have a job to keep my egg warm,
because of swoot-hunting, and I don't

suppose Og will sit on it.'

'I shan't,' said Og.

'You shouldn't, sir,' said Tum. 'It's no job for such a brave hunter as yourself.'

'But,' said Ut, 'there is one person who could incubate my egg for me, and its name is Tumblerum Wollycobble.'

And so, for the next six months (a gombrizil's egg takes a long time to hatch) Tumblerum lay under the mishmash trees, while safe and warm beneath its huge stomach lay Og and Ut's blue egg.

Partly to help pass the time and partly, it thought, to comfort the baby that was developing inside the egg, the slobbadunk took to singing lullabies in its deep voice. One of them went like this:

'How proud and pleased is Tumblerum,
To have, beneath its ample tum,
An egg so beautiful and blue.
O lovely egg! I think of you
Throughout each day, throughout each night.
Though you are hidden from my sight
As if I really had been blind,
You're never absent from my mind.
For though I haven't got a leg
To stand on, I've got Madam's egg!
Oh, what an honour, what a thrill
To hatch a baby gombrizil!'

All that time Ut worked hard collecting swoots for her babysitter, while Og went hunting for filigogs and hagafists and spuddicks for himself.

At last the day came when Tumblerum

Wollycobble suddenly felt a movement
beneath its huge stomach.

'Madam! Sir!' it cried, and as Ut and
Og hurried up, Tum slid slowly sideways,
to reveal a lot of broken blue eggshell
and a very small, newly hatched
gombrizil.

Og and Ut held legs.

'Our baby!' said Ut.

'Is it a boy?' asked Og.

'Don't know,' said Ut.

'Sir! Madam! Why not ask it?' said Tum.

So they did.

The baby gombrizil looked at them.

'I'm a girl,' she said. 'Who are you?'

'I'm Og, your daddy,' said Og.

'And I'm Ut, your mummy,' said Ut.

The baby looked at Tumblerum Wollycobble.

'What are you?' she said.

'I'm just a humble slobbadunk, miss.'

'What's your name?'

'Tum.'

'Well,' said the baby gombrizil, 'you've certainly got a lovely warm tummy, Tum. Thank you very much for hatching me.'

'It was a pleasure, miss.'

'Can I call you Uncle Tum? Or should it be Auntie Tum?'

'Better just call me Tum, miss.'

'But what are we going to call *you*?' said Og and Ut to their newly hatched daughter. 'It has to be short, mind. All gombrizils have short names.'

'Okay,' said the baby.

'Excuse me, miss,' said Tum, 'but do you mean that's what we are to call you?'

'Okay?' said the baby. 'Yes. Fine. I'm Okay,' and all four of them looked happily at one another under the mishmash trees.

Chapter Five

Og and Ut were bewitched by their baby daughter. They thought she was quite beautiful and spoiled her rotten. She was, after all, their only child, for a female gombrizil never lays more than one egg in her life, so that each and every baby hatched is an only child.

Ut taught Okay nice manners, and Og

taught her to hunt. Soon Okay was chasing spuddicks and catching small things like baby swoots. Most of these Okay ate, but she always stored a few in her tiny pouch to give to Tumblerum Wollycobble, who thought her the most wonderful thing in the world. She was the apple of its eye, and it was happier than it had ever been before.

Once, it thought, *I was a lonely old slobbadunk, friendless and a martyr to indigestion. Now I have two good pals, kindly Ut and brave handsome Og, and, above all, there is lovely little Okay. I think of her as my own baby. After all, I hatched her.*

As for Okay herself, she was, of course, fond of her parents, but it was the slobbadunk who was her great

friend. *Six months*, she thought, *I spent underneath Tum's warm tummy when I was an egg.* 'How good of it to brood me for so long, I can't thank it enough,' she would say to herself as she carefully withdrew a small succulent swoot from her pouch and popped it into the slobbadunk's round rubbery mouth.

Mostly, Tumblerum was fed – on large swoots – by Ut, though sometimes, on a

good hunting day, Og might bring
home a soft-shelled hagafist, or a filigog,
or a spuddick, as a present for the
slobbadunk. Tum was always touched
that Og had thought of it, but it was still
a vegetarian at heart. Swoots had to be
eaten for its digestion, but Tum liked
slippysloppy grass best of all.

Og's presents were never wasted. Ut
and Okay polished them off.

Life was good under the mishmash
trees.

Until the night of the Great Storm.

Throughout the previous day the
weather – which had been hot and dry
for some time – had seemed to be on
the change. By evening, the wind had

risen and the sky had filled
with dark scudding clouds.

As night fell, the three gombrizils and
the slobbadunk settled down as usual
under the mishmash trees. That is to say,
Og and Ut went to sleep side by side in
a big nest of leaves, the claw of Ut's
seventh leg tucked into Og's pouch in a
friendly, comforting kind of way. As for
Tumblerum Wollycobble, it slept at the
foot of the biggest mishmash tree, and

under its huge fat warm stomach slept
Okay. But round about midnight all of
them woke with a start at a sudden
deafening crash of thunder, followed by
blinding flashes of lightning. A howling
wind was flattening the slippysloppy
grass, over which the filigogs came
hopping wildly. The hagafists and the
long-eared spuddicks dashed down their
burrows, the strollops flew screeching
out of the trees, and only the swoots,
under their large flat stones, were safe
from the fury of the storm.

'Hold my leg, Ut, I'm scared!' shouted
Og, and he began to cry.

But then suddenly there came, right
above their heads, a creaking, groaning,
tearing noise as a huge branch of the

biggest of the mishmash trees split, broke off and fell, right on top of Tumblerum Wollycobble, the slobbadunk. It knocked the wind out of its body with a noise that sounded like the loudest of those burps which it no longer made.

Chapter Six

As quickly as it had started, the Great
Storm passed, the wind dropped, and
the strollops flew back into the treetops.

Ut had only one thought – her precious
daughter.

'Okay!' she cried. 'Where are you? Are
you okay, Okay?' But answer came there
none.

'Oh, stop snivelling, Og,' said Ut, 'and come and help me find her.'

Then she saw the fallen branch.

Then she saw what it had fallen on.

'Oh, Tum!' she cried. 'Are you all right?' And in answer she heard the slobbadunk's deep tones.

'No, madam,' it said. 'I can't say I am.'

'Are you badly hurt?'

'Bruised, madam, without doubt,' said

Tum, 'but even the biggest branch cannot break my bones.'

'Why not?'

'I haven't got any.'

'Oh,' said Ut. 'Oh, good. But oh, where is my little Okay?'

'Yes,' said Og, who had stopped crying now that the storm was past. 'Where is she?'

'Underneath me, brave sir,' said Tum.

'Well get off her then!'

'I cannot, sir. I am pinned down.'

'Oh, Ut!' said Og. 'What can we do?'

'Get that branch off Tum, of course,' replied Ut.

Both gombrizils reached out with their seventh legs and hooked their claws into the big branch and pulled with all their might, straining backwards with their other twelve legs. But they were not strong enough to move it.

'Stay here with Tum,' said Ut to Og. 'I'm going for help.' And she set off under the mishmash trees in a series of huge hops.

Generally, gombrizils like to keep themselves to themselves, but they will rally round in a crisis, and before long Ut brought back nine more gombrizils, three other pairs and a family of father, mother and a male child. All of them fastened their seventh legs on to the branch.

'When I say "Pull!",' shouted Og, 'we all pull.' And he did and they did, and Tumblerum Wollycobble managed, somehow, to inflate its big bruised body, and the branch rolled off.

'Quickly, Tum!' screeched Ut. 'Get off my little girl!'

With a great effort the slobbadunk managed to slide itself sideways, and there, all eleven gombrizils could see, was the figure of Okay, standing on all her seven legs and looking at them with her three eyes.

'Gosh!' she said. 'It wasn't half hot under there.'

'Oh, darling!' cried Og and Ut together. 'Are you all right?'

'I think so,' said Okay. 'What happened?'

'A big branch fell on Tum,' they said.

'Oh, Tum!' cried Okay. 'Are *you* all right?'

The slobbadunk stared fondly at her with its one large green eye in the middle of its forehead, and opened its round rubbery mouth and answered, 'Yes, miss.'

'Are you hurt?' asked Okay.

'A bit bruised, that's all,' said Tum.

It turned its eye upon all the other

gombrizils and said in its deep voice,
'My thanks to you all, ladies and
gentlemen, for rescuing me.'

'Yes, thank you!' cried Og and Ut with
one voice.

'As long as your daughter's okay,' the
rescuers said.

'She is, she is, it's her name!' said Og
and Ut, and Tum's green eye glistened.

Now the other three pairs of
gombrizils made off, and the family
of father, mother and male child were
about to follow, when the youngster
hopped up to Okay. He was just the
same size as she was.

'Is your name really Okay?' he asked.
'Yes.'
'Mine's Wow.'

'Wow!' said Okay.

'Hope we meet again,' he said.

'Me too.'

After the other family had gone, and Okay was comforting Tum by scratching its fat sides very gently with her seventh leg (which made it rumble softly with pleasure), Ut said to Og, 'Nice boy, didn't you think?'

'Huh!' said Og. 'Going to marry her

before long, I suppose you're thinking!'

'Why not?' said Ut. 'I quite fancy being a grandmother one day.

All was quiet now.

The filigogs hopped back, and the hagafists and the spuddicks came up out of their burrows, and in the treetops, the strollops cooed contentedly. Under their large flat stones, the swoots cooed contentedly and fatly, waiting, though they knew it not, to become food for the gombrizils and for Tumblerum Wollycobble, the slobbadunk.

'Feeling better, Tum?' Okay asked it.

'Much better, thank you, miss.'

'I won't always be a miss,' Okay said. 'One of these days I'll be a missus.'

'Wow!' said Tum.

Okay stretched out her seventh and longest leg, the one that grew beneath her chin, and gently scratched Tumblerum Wollycobble under where its chin would have been if it had had one.

'But you, Tum,' she said, 'will always be my best friend.'

Chapter Seven

Life under the mishmash trees went on pleasantly. Wow, the boy gombrizil, often came to see Okay and they would play together all day long. It was fun to chase the strollops when they came down to the ground to pick up fallen freeble fruits, but their three favourite games were probably Leap-filigog,

Hop-spuddick and Tag-a-hagafist.

Tumblerum Wollycobble too, was always pleased to see Wow, who never failed to be very nice to it and often brought it little gifts of swoots.

But the problem with life going on pleasantly is that time seems to pass very quickly, and one fine day, many years later, Ut looked at Og and thought how old he had become. 'Not that he isn't still the handsomest of gombrizils,' she said to herself, 'but he's not so good on his legs as he used to be and his bones are a bit creaky.'

At much the same time Og looked at Ut and said to himself, 'Oh dear, she was such a pretty girl and now, well, she's showing her age and no mistake.'

Okay was by now grown up, as was her boyfriend, Wow, but Og and Ut knew that there was a long time yet to wait before they could hope – if things went right – to become grandparents.

As for Tumblerum Wollycobble, life went on as usual. Slobbadunks are very, very long-lived and what's more, they continue to look much the same, however old they are. Tum was especially healthy,

probably because, unlike the other slobbadunks, it was no longer a martyr to indigestion. Og and Ut still brought it occasional swoots, but they were now too slow to catch much for themselves, and Okay and Wow started to do most of the hunting. Between them, they caught hagafists and spuddicks and filigogs for Og and Ut, and brought

home in their pouches regular rations of
swoots for their great friend Tum.

But then one day something happened
under the mishmash trees that made
everyone very happy.

Og and Ut were lying side by side
in their nest of leaves, gently and
affectionately scratching each other with
one of their many legs, and idly watching

the strollops above feeding on the freeble fruits. Tum was digesting (easily, these days) a huge meal of slippysloppy grass.

Then along came Okay and her boyfriend. Wow marched up to the nest and said to Og, 'Could I have a word, sir?'

'Certainly, my boy,' replied Og. 'What's the trouble?'

'No trouble, sir,' said Wow. 'At least I hope not. I have come to ask for your daughter's claw in marriage. We wish to wed.'

'Please, Daddy!' said Okay. 'Can we?'

'Of course, darling!' shouted Ut before her husband could reply.

'Of course, darling,' echoed Og, and to Wow he said, 'I shall expect you to

take the greatest
care of my little
girl.'

As for Tum, its
round rubbery
mouth opened and out of it came a
joyful sound of great excitement and
satisfaction, a sound like 'Wheeeeeeee!'
while the one green eye in the middle of
its forehead glistened with tears of
happiness.

'Congratulations, sir and madam!' said
the slobbadunk, once Okay and Wow had
gone off happily together. 'Now you can
look forward to becoming grandparents.'

'We'll have to look a long way forward,'
said Og. 'She's very young.'

'Time will pass,' said Tum, 'and when

the happy event does occur, I wonder if I might beg the greatest of favours?'

'What?' said Og.

'May I keep the egg warm, as I did for your daughter?'

'You'll have to ask her,' said Og.

'I'm sure she'll say yes, Tum,' said Ut. 'You made such a good job of hatching her.'

Okay and Wow made their way out from the shelter of the mishmash trees in a daze of happiness as the strollops screeched above. Each put a claw into the other's pouch as they hopped along side by side.

'Oh, Wow!' said Okay. 'Just think, we're going to be married!'

'If that's okay by you, Okay,' Wow replied.

'Oh, Wow! It is! We've always had such fun together!'

And they had too.

As children, they had spent hours playing games like Clawball, where they kicked an unripe freeble fruit about, or different athletic competitions – long jump and high jump (which Wow generally won) and races (in which Okay

was usually the winner).

Later, as teenage gombrizils, they hunted together, at first just to get swoots for Tumblerum Wollycobble, but then later, as Og and Ut grew older, the youngsters caught food for them.

The slow, soft-shelled hagafists were easy prey, but the long-eared spuddicks and especially the filigogs that hopped swiftly by, their busy tails curled over their backs, were much more difficult for a single gombrizil to catch. Two gombrizils working together, though, were a different matter and, as Okay was fond of saying, 'Wow and I make a great team.'

Sometimes they would run the spuddicks and filigogs down, taking

turns in the chase, but mainly they relied upon ambush.

One of them (Okay, let's say) would hide in the deep slippysloppy grass, for example, and then Wow would drive the chosen creature towards her. Okay would jump out on the juicy spuddick or fat filigog and catch it easily.

But, of course, they never forgot Tum, and each day they would collect pouchfuls of the fattest, most succulent swoots for their friend.

They were talking of Tum as they hopped along together on this, the day of their engagement.

'It hatched you, didn't it?' Wow said.

'Yes,' replied Okay. 'The dear thing sat on me for six months, Mummy told me. Who hatched you, Wow, d'you know?'

'My dad,' said Wow.

'Not your mum?'

'No. She told him to do it, so he did.'

'When I lay an egg,' Okay said, 'will you sit on it?'

'No fear!' said Wow.

'What, you're going to make me sit on it for six months?'

'No,' said Wow. 'When the time comes, we'll ask old Tum.'

Chapter Eight

As the young gombrizils walked and talked, old Tum was asleep under the mishmash trees. Its large meal of slippysloppy grass was taking quite a bit of digesting, and when it woke, it found that Og and Ut had gone off together, and that it was alone and still rather hungry.

Tum slithered to its larder, a shallow hole between the roots of a big mishmash tree. This storeplace was the idea of Okay and Wow, and in it they put supplies of spare swoots.

Though it was easiest for Tum to have a swoot popped into that round rubbery mouth by one or other of the young gombrizils, it could still manage to feed itself, if left alone, thanks to this larder. It would peer in with that one green eye in the middle of its forehead, to make

sure that there were swoots inside (there always were) and then it would stick its mouth down into the hole and suck up swoot after swoot.

Now, its hunger satisfied, Tumblerum Wollycobble decided to take a little modest exercise.

In the old days its progress would have been marked by an endless series of loud belches, but now its digestion, thanks to the swoots, was perfect. Certainly its mouth opened as it slid along, but not to emit a burp.

Instead there came from that round rubbery hole a kind of whistling noise, which sounded rather plaintive but which was, in fact, joyful.

Tum was whistling from pure

happiness on that sunny morning as it
thought with fondness of the family of
gombrizils that had adopted it.

Og, it remembered, had long ago
pretended to be frightened – ridiculous
for such a brave handsome creature.

Ut had always been kind to it.

As for Okay, Tumblerum Wollycobble
thought of her as a sort of daughter and of

Wow, therefore, as a kind of son-in-law.

Then, suddenly, it saw them both, hopping happily along together. Each of them had their seventh claw in the other one's pouch, for this is how gombrizils hold hands.

'Hullo, Tum!' they cried.

Oh, thought the slobbadunk, *should I ask them if I can hatch their egg now? Or would it be better to wait a while?* But before it could make up its mind, Okay hopped right up close and stroked its fat back with one of her legs and said, 'Tum, dear, we've something to ask you. Will you do us a great favour?'

'Of course, miss, of course, young sir!' said Tum. 'What is it?'

'When the time comes for me to lay

my egg,' said Okay, 'will you hatch it, as
you did me?'

Tum's one and only green eye glistened
with sudden tears.

'Of course, miss!' it cried.

'Great!' they said.

'And please,' said Okay, 'drop the
"miss" and the "young sir" and call us by

our proper names from now on. You are our special friend, you know.'

'Okay, Okay,' said Tumblerum Wollycobble joyfully.

Chapter Nine

The years passed for the happy family
under the mishmash trees, and everyone,
especially Okay, spent a lot of time
wondering when a very special egg would
be laid. They wondered when Wow
would be a father, and when Og and Ut
would become the grandparents they
longed to be, and when Tum would begin

to hatch it.

Each year Okay grew nearer to middle age, the time when female gombrizils come into lay. Each year, obviously, Og and Ut grew older and more anxious to set eyes on that grandson or granddaughter. They remained in good health, however, despite their age, thanks to a generous diet. Their son-in-law was a mighty hunter, and both the old gombrizils feasted royally on plentiful supplies of tender young hagafists and juicy spuddicks and fine fat filigogs.

'Wow, dear,' said Okay one day. 'I think I may be coming into lay before too long. I feel ever so full.'

'Oh, darling!' cried Wow. 'How marvellous! Will it be a boy or a girl, I

wonder? What do you think?'

'I'm not sure,' replied Okay.
'Sometimes I think it's the one and
sometimes the other. Better not say
anything to Mummy or Daddy yet.'

'What about Tum?' asked Wow.

'Well, it doesn't need to know until
the egg is laid.'

Which it was, not many days later.

Okay and Wow had their own bed of leaves under the mishmash trees, some little distance from Og and Ut's, and early one morning Wow was woken by Okay saying, 'Go and get some swoots for Tum, there's a good boy.'

'What, this early?' yawned Wow. 'Can't

it wait a bit?'

'No, it can't!' said Okay in an angry voice. 'Now push off, do.'

'Females,' said Wow to himself as he staggered off into the dawn. 'There's no understanding them.'

But he understood right enough when he came back with a pouchful of swoots, for there was his wife standing proudly over the nest, while beneath her, in between her seven long legs, was a big, beautiful, bright-blue egg!

'Oh, dearest!' cried Wow. 'You've done it! Are you all right! How do you feel?'

'To tell the truth,' replied Okay, 'I still feel full.'

She shifted uncomfortably.

'What can you mean?' asked Wow, as his

wife settled down again upon the nest.

'Look the other way!' said Okay sharply.

Obediently, Wow did as he was bidden. Then he heard a kind of grunt and then a sort of plop.

'You can turn round now,' said Okay, and when Wow did so, she stood up again and there in the nest were two eggs, side by side. One was blue, the other was pink.

Wow was speechless. Gombrizils only ever have one child, his mother had told

him, yet now it seemed he was the
father of . . . twins!

'Go and fetch Tum,' said Okay.

When the slobbadunk eventually
arrived, Okay stepped from the nest.

'What do you see, Tum?' she asked.

Tumblerum Wollycobble's one green
eye nearly popped out of its head.

'Two, miss! I mean, two, Okay!' it

gasped. 'However . . .? I mean, your mother and father told me that gombrizils never lay more than one egg.'

'Well,' said Okay, 'Mummy and Daddy were wrong, it seems. We were all wrong. But are you willing to sit on both of them?'

'Of course, Okay,' said Tum. 'It makes no difference to me. I'll be on duty for six months anyway.'

'Dear, kind, Tum,' said Okay. 'But promise me you won't say anything to my mum and dad. They'll think you're sitting on one egg, and if anything goes wrong, I mean, if only one should hatch out, they'll never know.'

'Nothing is going to go wrong,' said Tum firmly. 'Shall I start now?'

'Yes, please,' said Okay.

'Jolly good show, Tum,' said Wow.

The slobbadunk looked thoughtfully at the two gombrizil eggs in the nest.

'Different colours,' it said. 'Do you think that perhaps . . . ?'

'Yes,' said Okay, 'with a bit of luck. Blue for a girl, we know – the egg you hatched me from was blue – and pink for a boy.'

And would you believe it, that's how things turned out.

Chapter Ten

Six months dragged by, maddeningly slowly for the proud parents and the expectant grandparents, while Tumblerum Wollycobble sat stolidly upon the nest, well fed by Okay and Wow on swoots and on supplies of slippysloppy grass that they scratched up with their sharp claws.

The strollops perched above, dropping occasional ripe freeble fruits, which were  fed to Tum, and waiting to carry news of the birth to every other gombrizil and slobbadunk, hagafist, spuddick and filigog. When it happened, only the swoots, lying fatly under their big flat stones, would not know straightaway.

As he had while brooding Okay, Tum
sang to the two eggs beneath him.

  '*Oh, what a bit of luck! Just think,*
  There's two of you, one blue, one pink,
  We'll simply have to wait and see
  What sort of Gombrizils you'll be.
  I wonder, will you both be hes?
  Or will the pair of you be shes?
  Or will it be one girl, one boy,
  To give your mum and dad such joy,
  One like Okay and one like Wow?
  There isn't any knowing how
  It all will end when out you come
  From underneath your loving Tum.'

For the rest of their lives Og and Ut
would never forget the hatching day.

They were woken early by Wow calling, 'Quick! Come quick!' and they hopped slowly and sleepily after him.

'Oh, Og!' said Ut. 'I hope it's a boy, brave and handsome like you.'

'Oh, Ut!' said Og. 'I hope it's a girl, quick and clever as you are.'

They came to the nest where Okay was waiting and where Tum still lay, its bulk concealing whatever was there. Then the slobbadunk slowly slithered out of the mess of brushed leaves and broken eggshell, some blue, some pink, to reveal not one, but two tiny gombrizils.

'Say hello to Grandpa and Grandma,' said Okay, and the babies squeaked.

'Two!' said Og in utter amazement.

'What are they?' said Ut.

'Gombrizils,' replied Og.

'No, no,' said Ut. 'I mean – are they girls or boys or what?'

'Ask them, Mummy,' said Okay.

Ut bent down over the nest.

'Listen, children,' she said softly, and she pointed to one of the twins. 'What are you?' she asked.

'I'm a girl,' the baby replied.

Ut pointed to the other, which had a little bit of pink shell still stuck on its back.

'And you?'

'I'm a boy,' said the other baby.

'Many congratulations, Wow, my lad,' said Og to his son-in-law.

'Okay, darling,' said Ut to her daughter. 'No gombrizil has ever done such a thing before!'

'I only laid the eggs, Mummy,' said Okay. 'It was Tum who hatched them.'

'A privilege,' said Tumblerum Wollycobble in its deep voice, while above their heads the strollops, eager to spread the amazing news, flew screeching out of the mishmash trees.

What a happy family it was that now lived under those trees!

After much discussion Okay and Wow

had settled upon names for the newly hatched twins, names which must, of course, be pretty short ones. The girl was to be called Bluebell, the boy Pinky, and each was already hopping happily about on its seven little legs.

It was not long after that memorable day when the twins first brought presents for their grandparents.

Bluebell pulled out from her little pouch a tiny, soft-shelled hagafist and Pinky had speared a small swoot.

'Oh, you clever darlings!' cried Ut. 'You're going to be great hunters like your daddy!'

'And your grandpa,' said Og, with his mouth full of hagafist.

Ut picked up Pinky's swoot and

hopped slowly over to a particular leafy hollow under a particular mishmash tree, which was where Tumblerum Wollycobble, the slobbadunk, could usually be found.

It looked up as she approached, staring fondly at her out of that one large green eye.

'Like a swoot, Tum?' she asked.

'Oh, thank you, madam,' said the

slobbadunk. 'You are so good to me.'

'Well, you're one of the family,' Ut said. 'You hatched Okay for me and you hatched Bluebell and Pinky for Okay.'

Even as she spoke, the twins appeared.

'Morning, Uncle Tum,' said Bluebell, and 'Morning, Auntie Tum,' said Pinky, and off they hopped.

The slobbadunk watched them for a moment and then it turned to Ut and opened that round rubbery mouth.

'Oh, madam, dear madam,' it said. 'To think of all that you have done for me since first we met. You helped me when I thought I had gone blind; you cured my indigestion; you saved me on the day of the Great Storm. How can I ever thank you enough?'

'No need, Tum,' said Ut. 'It is I who have to thank you. You mean so much to my grandchildren, to my daughter, to my son-in-law, to my husband, and most of all, to me. You are my best friend.'

A large tear ran out of Tum's green eye. Its round rubbery mouth opened, but no words came out, only a deep sigh of content.

In happy silence, Ut, the gombrizil, and Tumblerum Wollycobble, the slobbadunk, enjoyed one another's company under the mishmash trees.